J.M. GOKEY

The Hatebug

Contents

Author's Note

This is extreme horror, emphasis on EXTREME. If you're mentally stable and not a fan of profanity, this probably isn't the story for you. Proceed with that warning in mind, and enjoy!

Before

"Night-night Stell-bell, don't let the *Hatebug* bite."

Allen kissed his daughter's forehead before pulling the covers up her neck. He made his way to the baby pink bedroom door that matched *everything else* in the room. As his hand grazed against the surprisingly *not* pink light switch, his daughter tossed the covers away and sat up.

"Dada, what's a *Hatebug*?"

Stella had been three years old. She was oh so curious now, a little *too* curious, he thought to himself. The question itself shouldn't have surprised him. It also shouldn't have caused his chest to pound, or his mouth to dry up. A thick layer of sweat formed above his thick brows. Allen wiped the sweat away with the back of his hand. He bit his tongue once, then twice, waiting for enough saliva to pool inside of his mouth to be able to swallow. Once he was satisfied with the pathetic amount of liquid, he did swallow. His efforts were for nothing, his mouth and throat remained bone dry.

Allen had been so distracted trying to prevent himself from cracking, that he almost didn't notice the wide watchful eyes of his daughter. Somehow, even with her young age, she recognized the fear on his face, maybe even, the fear inside of his racing heart.

Fear of the *real* Hatebug, not the silly story kids told to each other around Halloween bonfires just before a long night of wetting the bed.

Allen first heard of the Hatebug as a young child, on Halloween night, gathered around his parent's pleather couch. It originated as a Halloween story, a tale, a legend, whatever the hell you wanted to call it. Each Halloween night the Hatebug would emerge from its *slumber* to search for a target.

Some say the creature is really a demon disguised as a harm—less bug, sent up from the fiery depths of Hell, the devil himself whispering orders into its concious.

Just one bite from the little critter was all it took.

Suddenly your life would fall apart.

You might lose your job.

You might lose a loved one — *a brother.*

In the kiddie version, the creature targeted children who ate too much candy, a story made up by parents trying to avoid sick call-outs from school and hyperactive sugar monsters.

However, it was not a fuzzy little spider with enormous, adorable eyes and a great big smile. It was also not a tiny bug that pinches bare toes at the edge of beds. Most importantly, love, laughter, light, and eating only a moderate amount of sweets did not in fact scare the true Hatebug away.

Allen had never seen the Hatebug with his own eyes.

He prayed he never would.

But he had seen the damage the parasite could cause years ago, he was certain of it.

All he knew for sure was that it was a bug, but not any typical bug. This bug could destroy your life with its bite. Maybe, it didn't even have to bite you. It preys on mental weakness and those with everything to lose.

The Hatebug makes you wish you never existed.

Allen liked to believe he was a good father. He had always been kind, and fair, and loving. He did not and never would coddle his children, though. He chose never to lie to his daughter, even when the answer might not be what she wanted to hear.

Tonight would be no different.

Especially when the truth behind the story of the Hatebug had already made their family victims nearly ten years prior.

Allen's older brother, Steve, was bitten by the creature, or so he believed. No one ever saw the deep pricks in his pale neck but him. He knew what he saw, his eyes did not deceive him.

Steve had been in his late thirties. He was handsome, had a full head of hair (unlike Allen's own shiny bald head), a beautiful wife, and three adorable boys. The week before *it* happened, he landed his dream job as a Program Manager for NASA. Steve had it all, his life had been everything he ever wished for and more.

Then out of the blue *Steve* decided to quit his dream job, crash his car, take a dump on their parent's front lawn, brutally murder his wife and kids, and then blow his brains out — in that order.

Allen had been the one to find all five of their mangled corpses.

Earlier that day their mother called Allen. She was worried about Steve. In a panicked state, she brought Allen up to speed on his brother's sudden erratic behavior, begging for Allen to just pop in and check on him.

Steve had always been the favorite, he remembered rolling his eyes while he listened to his mother go on and on.

Allen was jealous of his brother, that was no secret. That jealousy only grew over the years. Things always seemed to go in Steve's favor, but that week things were going a little *too well* in his brother's life, while Allen on the other hand, struggled to make ends meet, surviving on ramen noodles and tap water.

Shit, he had his electricity shut off more times than he could count on one hand.

So what if Steve was having a *bad day*?

When Allen finally moseyed his way up to Steve's front door, he heard the final gunshot. He was too late.

Allen never once believed that his brother would take his own life, let alone his entire family, even if the police officers ruled it a murder-suicide before they even stepped inside the house.

Allen never did let the unusual mark on his brother's neck go, even if no one believed him. It was an image he would remember for the rest of his life. Even his own wife called bullshit, so eventually he kept the theory to himself all together.

Any proof of the creature's hold on his brother was long gone before the police arrived. But Allen knew what he saw. He knew what was responsible.

It haunted him to this day.

For years he searched for answers. Every lead led him in circles, amounting to nothing. Even with the lack of information he possessed, the facts of the matter pointed to something otherworldly, something evil.

"Dada?"

The sound of Stella's voice snapped him back to reality.

"There is always some truth to every story, my sweet girl."

The Hatebug

*B*lood, so much blood.

I woke up to the sound of a crash — glass I think. It scared me so badly that I wet the bed. I put on my slippers, the bunny ear ones, and I went to go look for my mom and dad.

I ran to their bedroom first, I knocked on the door, but there was no answer. The door was ajar, open just enough to peek inside. I saw my mom's blonde hair peeking out from underneath the blanket. I figured she was sleeping.

I didn't know at the time that she was already dead.

Raped.

Mutilated

Tortured for hours while I slept soundly.

. . . I didn't want to wake her, she worked so hard all day. I didn't see my dad. I assumed he might be awake, in the kitchen, with the cups and plates — all glass. I closed the door and went to go look for him.

I was so scared going down the long hallway. My stomach felt weird. Something wasn't right. The closer I got to the kitchen, the more I started to hear a voice. Crying. Someone was crying in the kitchen. My dad was crying in the kitchen, alone, sitting on the floor. His hands ran through his sweat-drenched hair, tugging, pulling.

He couldn't see me yet. I peeked around the corner. The longer I watched, the more I began to regret leaving my room at all.

There was a knife on the floor by his feet, covered in red. At the moment I thought it might be jam, maybe he was making a sandwich.

It was an innocent thought.

But then I realized that the red was all over him. He was painted in that dark red substance just at the start of coagulation. His hands were stained, his face, and especially his once-white t-shirt.

I was so quiet.

He started talking, talking to himself. He spoke as if there were someone else in the kitchen with him, but I didn't see anyone.

"N-no . . . p-please . . ." The first voice begged. It was a voice I could recognize anywhere, my daddy.

"Let's get this over with you stupid pathetic fucker." The second voice spoke — deeper, harsher. The words came out of my dad's mouth, but it wasn't him speaking.

The voice was something darker, more sinister. It was hoarse as if it belonged to a longtime smoker.

The floor betrayed me, it creaked beneath my feet.

There was no escaping this, he heard me, both of them heard me.

My dad started crying harder, so hard he choked on phlegm as he yelled, "Stella run, run baby, go to Mrs. Donohue's house — NOW!"

My dad never yelled in front of me, that was the first and last time I ever heard him raise his voice at all.

I didn't run until I saw him pick up the knife.

Then, I ran as fast as my little legs would let me, but he was faster.

"Get over here you piss-soaked little cunt, I wonder if you're as sweet as your mommy. Be a good girl and let me have a taste, hm?"

He grabbed my arm, digging his nails into my skin. Blood gushed out, he licked his lips, moaning at the scent of it. He swung me around, the most wicked smile I have ever seen to this day on his face.

I didn't quite understand what death was at the time, but I knew something bad was going to happen.

Then his face shifted again. I saw a flash of my real dad. He mouthed, "I'm sorry", and then he slit his throat right in front of me.

"— Stella, let's remember that the only one there with you that night was your father. You can not begin to heal until you can accept the truth of what happened. Children who have experienced trauma as you have tend to block out the bad, some even replace those memories with fiction. Your father brutally murdered your mother, he did unspeakable things while you slept, and then he proceeded to rape and mutilate her corpse for hours."

Stella shook her head, "My father would *never* hurt anyone, not like that."

"Alright then . . ." The older woman pushed her black-framed glasses farther up the bridge of her nose and crossed her legs. "Tell me then, Stella, who do you think killed your mother that night, and your father?"

That question always pissed her off. Maybe it wasn't the question, but more so the condescending tone that followed suit. It was not one she *liked* to answer.

Stella didn't know *what* killed her parents.

She wasn't delusional, she knew and accepted that her father killed himself, she accepted that years ago. He killed himself to protect her from the thing that had a hold on him. He made the ultimate sacrifice to protect her from the *thing* that killed her mother.

It was not a person.

It may have been something otherworldly, something supernatural.

It could have been anything.

Stella, however, did not want to be admitted to a grippy-sock vacation quite yet. So instead of her real theories, she said what she always did, "I don't know."

The timer rang.

End of another *successful* session.

"Well, I'll see ya next time Doctor Stevey."

"Doctor *Stevens* — Wait before you leave, I have a question I would like you to reflect on until our next session. I would like us to discuss what your father may have said to you before he . . . well, see you next Wednesday, Stella. *Happy Halloween!*"

Stella nodded and tried to smile, but it wouldn't form. Instead, she just stared blankly at the peppered grey hairs sprouting from the woman's perfect little head, trying to overthrow the blonde she worked so hard to maintain. Botox was also one hell of a thing.

"Yup, next Wednesday."

Stella wasn't sure why she still came to each appointment. Every Wednesday for the past three years she sat and talked to the old cunt.

The few friends she still had, convinced her to start going. She listened. Friends were hard to come by, she knew that all too well. No one knew how to be friends with the *trauma* kids. It would be good for her, they said. So far she hadn't found any *good* in it. But, it was part of her routine now.

Her friends meant well.

They cared for her, they looked at her as if she were a normal person, at least most of the time.

Others all around her, for the majority of her life, saw her only as *the troubled one, an orphan, broken.*

It would take more than two dead parents to break her.

* * *

Stella left the dingy office building behind, slamming the door of her piece of shit '99 civic shut. The body was rusted and the transmission was on its way out, but it got her from point A to B without a hitch.

Hands on the wheel, she stared blankly at the empty parking lot in front of her through hazel eyes.

Technically she had nowhere to be. However, the thought of going straight home made her stomach churn. It was October 31st, better known as Halloween.

Not only was it the anniversary of her parents dying, it also happened to be the day her friend Nick decided to turn her home into a fucking zoo every year.

Stella was too old to give a shit, her roommate Nick, however, was quite fond of the holiday.

Okay, he was a little *obsessed* with the day. Each year the fixation grew more and more *unhealthy.*

To any normal person, his antics would seem normal and fun. To her, it was uncomfortable.

The thought of sitting through another party full of sluts dressed as cats and nuns made her want to hurl the pumpkin spice latte that refused to settle in her already uneasy stomach.

Lucky for Nick, Stella had no money and all of her friends would be at this party.

Stella turned the key in the ignition, jumping at the deep rumble of the exhaust. "Just stick with me til I win the lottery," she groaned.

She would never win the lottery, but still, she couldn't afford for the shitbox to crap out on her just yet.

Foot on the gas, the car inched forward. A sharp pain, similar to that of hot metal against flesh, tore into her neck causing her to slam on the brakes. The car jolted to a stop. Her hand smacked against the source as she swore left and right.

Stella didn't want to look, it felt fucking gnarly, so it most likely looked the part. She couldn't help but flinch at the thought, she'd always been so queasy with that shit.

Stella could handle most things.

Ghosts — *Sure.*

Vomit — *Yup.*

Snakes — *Whatever.*

Death — *Absolutely.*

But, insects, bugs, anything creepy-crawly — *Fuck no.*

All of the signs led to the same unsettling conclusion, something definitely bit her neck and it probably wasn't some smoking hot vampire.

Her heart raced in her chest, and consequently, her mouth dried up. Nerves took over, and she couldn't help but think to herself, *maybe if I don't look it never happened.*

Wishful thinking.

When the pain radiating from the spot right below her jaw grew more painful instead of just going away like she hoped, she decided to put her big girl pants on and take a look.

As the dark of the night crept in, she could only see so much in the mirror. She used the light from the screen of her phone to spot two quarter-size lumps side by side, both red and swollen. They were so close to her throat, her lymph nodes, her fucking brain.

A few minutes had gone by now.

She was still alive, that was something.

Her eyes scanned the entirety of the car. She saw no bug corpse. And thank fuck, she did not see the body of anything larger than an insect. The skin around the unusually large bite was now an eyesore tomato red, small tinges of purple bruising slowly spread out from the initial zones.

Red and purple were better than brown and black and possible necrosis, so she had that going for her.

Stella swallowed once, then twice.

Suffering for years with a general anxiety disorder and the oh-so-lovely panic attacks that went hand in hand, she had a checklist to confirm her throat was not closing.

Still not satisfied by the fact that she could still swallow, she sang a random tune to confirm she could still talk. It was something along the lines of *fuck, fuck, fuckity, fuck.*

Her entire throat system seemed to be in working order.

Her neck hurt like a motherfucker, and quite honestly her head was starting to hurt a bit, but she didn't think she would die, not immediately at least.

Stella took one more good look in the mirror, the pain was now subsiding, but the two purple orbs attached to her neck still looked awful.

At least she didn't need a costume now.

* * *

The entire street was full, cars parked back to back like sardines. Stella muttered a few *fucks* and *motherfuckers* under her breath before she finally spotted her roommate Nick and her boyfriend Ian standing side by side in an empty spot directly in front of the house.

She pressed her fingers tightly against the bridge of her nose, trying to knead out the steadily building migraine.

She parked the car, hesitating slightly before getting out.

The two shitheads waiting for her eyed her eagerly, waiting to hear her always so *lovely* thoughts about the party. As usual, she wouldn't have anything nice to say.

I fucking hate Halloween, she muttered to herself.

Her shaky hands found the door handle. Before she could ease it open, she heard a voice.. It sounded as if it were right behind her, maybe even right into her ear. She was alone, she knew for certain she was alone. The voice was too close, too clear to have come from outside of the vehicle. The familiarity of the voice sent a wave of nausea over her.

Stella couldn't pinpoint it.

Burn it down

It had to have come from the radio. Or maybe it was all in her head.

Regardless, it was *probably* nothing.

"Love the costume, Stell, lovely as always." Nick teased, wincing as if waiting for her to smack him.

Nick wore a hot pink cropped tank with coordinating leggings and leg warmers — the *80's.*

Nick was snarky, clean, had a decent sense of humor, and most importantly — he was *really* into men. Overall he added up to being the perfect roommate, and a great friend, minus the over-the-top parties.

From the moment they met, Nick accepted her for the dumpster fire she was and took her in as family. Shit, she had even spent holidays with him and his parents.

It was hard enough growing up without parents. When the aunt who raised her also kicked the bucket a few years back, truly having no family struck a nerve.

Now she had Nick and Ian, and they were more than enough.

"Oh fuck off, Nick. Not a costume, just a bad day."

Ian wrapped an arm around her waist, getting a good look at her still-swollen neck. "Jesus, you look like shit, babe. What the fuck happened? Did that therapist finally rip you a new one, literally?"

Stella appreciated the half-assed concern, she did, just not the execution. She swatted his hand away and groaned. "I don't look *that* bad. Something bit me on the way over here, bugs have always loved my blood, I'll be fine."

Ian gave her the look, the *you've gotta be shitting me* look. "That car becomes more of a hazard every day, bugs now, huh?" He hadn't even gotten a good look at the pricks on her neck yet. Instead, he was referring to the dark purple bags under her eyes, the way her cheeks sunk into her face despite not losing any weight, even just the overall tone of her voice.

Ian pulled her in, a whisper in her ear. "I know this shit isn't your thing, but don't go getting sick on me now. I know today is a tough one, but we'll get through it together."

Stella nodded, staring blankly toward the front door, the entrance to Hell. Her migraine never dissipated, and now her heart raced — a feeling much different from her typical anxiety-driven body reaction.

Out of nowhere, for whatever reason, she felt *alive*, the kind of feeling she always imagined she would need to dip her toes into the world of hard drugs to experience.

Pure adrenaline raced through her veins.

She was suddenly ready to fucking *party*.

That deep, dark voice rang through clear as day yet again, *Let's have some fun.*

Ian watched her in awe. A feeling of dread washed over him. Stella would *never*. Never — not in a million years.

Illness wouldn't explain this.

His mind wandered to the various possibilities. She could be using, she had no track record of drugs as far as he knew, but it was still one avenue he could explore.

It made no fucking sense, but there she was dancing her ass off, mixing and mingling with the general population, he even saw her hug some random chick.

Ian decided to take action, pushing past small groups and cliques, and making his way through the zoo of partygoers. After a few annoyed looks and *watch it's*, he got close enough to get a good tug on her arm.

At first, she fought him off, shooing his hands off of her as if he were a fly, a nuisance.

Stella was throwing her ass back to *Thriller*, still dressed in an oversized *Nirvana* tee and a pair of gray joggers.

Practically every single young adult in the city was there, dressed in costume, watching her make a fucking fool of herself. Ian couldn't bear to watch any longer.

He yelled out her name, and screamed out a few rash words, it was no use. She couldn't hear him over the bass of the stereo. Or, she chose to ignore him. Either way, he gripped her arm tight now, tighter than he should have, tighter than he normally ever would. He expected her to flinch, to shoo him off, instead, she smiled.

It was more of a smirk, laced with seduction. It was one of those faces you only saw in private, a face too dangerous to flash around anywhere else. Especially, not at a party in the middle of a crowd of sweaty, horny, drunk motherfuckers.

The look kind of scared him.

It also kind of made his cock twitch.

A little of this, a little of that.

"Let's get out of here, go upstairs, get some air, anything. I'm worried about you."

Her face went blank as she mumbled in a voice he didn't recognize, "You should be."

* * *

Stella felt like she was on a bad trip. She was losing time, losing pieces of her day. She could see that she was walking up the staircase with Ian, steps she had taken a million times before.

They were not alone.

Someone else was with them, maybe *something* else.

I'm a little hungry, princess

Her stomach dropped, her skull itched. The voice came from inside of her, creeping up her very core. She had heard that voice earlier. It wasn't just a fluke. Something was inside of her.

Suddenly she felt very queasy.

Stella squeezed Ian's hand, he turned to face her, head cocked to the side. She tried to speak. She wanted so badly to scream that something was very wrong, but the words came out as a garbled mess.

It wouldn't let her warn him. It wouldn't let her do or say anything unless *it* wanted her to.

You catch on fast

Stella led him into her bedroom, slamming the door shut behind them. She could feel her body temperature rising. Her cheeks flushed, *hot, so hot.* As the temperature kept rising, she ripped her clothing off piece by piece.

Sure she was acting weird, but who was he to deny her? Sex was a hell of a lot better than venturing back downstairs and embarrassing herself.

Stella could only compare how she was feeling to going into a night thinking you're consuming a 20mg edible and instead you find out you ate 200mg. She was no longer in control of her body, not even her words. Instead, she was now *the watcher*.

Suck him dry, princess, the one in control ordered. It wasn't an *awful* idea, but not one of her own. Her body had no fight left, the parasite inched its flesh suit forward.

Stella pushed Ian's frame with a strength she definitely didn't have. Ian wasn't anywhere close to being considered *lanky*, yet his muscled frame fell back onto the bed without any hindrance.

She grinned at the sight before her, *Men are so fucking weak for a pretty face.*

Stella climbed on top of him, straddling him at his waist. Only her black lace panties separated her heat from the hard-on beneath her. She leaned into the warmth of his neck, planting soft kisses from his jaw down to the very edge of his boxers. Her fingers wandered beneath the elastic, a silent command.

Let's see what he's packing

Ian let a moan slip out, glancing down to see her big doe eyes staring back. He fucking loved her. And no, it wasn't the thought of knowing he was about to feel her mouth around him that influenced that feeling.

He really did love her.

Stella was in there somewhere, overwhelmed with a familiar feeling of dread.

Something bad was going to happen, *she* was going to be forced to do something awful to someone she loved.

She tried to fight, she wished he would just look at her, *really* look at her, and see it in her eyes to run.

He didn't.

He won't

Her mouth wrapped tightly around his hard cock. The frequent motion of friction rocked the bed. Ian let out sound after sound of pure ecstasy, oblivious of the creature she had become one with.

It waited patiently. *Closer, closer . . .*

It listened to the cues his body gave, waiting for that perfect moment right before he'd blow his load down her throat.

One . . . two . . . THREE!

Stella bit down, *hard*, cutting clean through the entirety of his dick right at the base with only her teeth. Metallic liquid filled her mouth in one great gush. She swallowed hard, desperately slurping each and every drop of his blood as if she had never drank such a delicacy before.

Ian screamed out so loud it could have pierced through the blaring music below them, a deep guttural yell fueled by the unbearable pain that slipped in through the adrenaline that numbed his system.

The sudden dismemberment, abruptly losing that piece of him, it sent his body into shock, he couldn't fathom what the hell had just happened.

Stella opened her mouth wide, letting what was left of his cock fall out with a wet *slap* against his blood-stained torso.

Ian, still in that near-paralyzed state, stared up at her with both fear and confusion in his eyes.

Stella licked each of her fingers, sucking off each drop of blood that she could.

"You taste so good, baby. So damn good." She lunged at him, baring her teeth like some rabid animal. Her teeth sliced so easily

through the sensitive skin at his neck, it amazed her. Once again she devoured his blood, its flavor so rich, so sweet, she moaned through each gulp.

His body wriggled beneath her, she felt a familiar heat building through her core.

A feeling she started to chase.

Stella's panties were drenched at the feeling of his pathetic life slipping away. His body thrashed violently as she drank, but the grip of her thighs around him was too strong, he couldn't push her off of him.

The fight only made it that much more exciting.

As he took his final gargled breath, she exploded all over him.

The creature refused to let her feel remorse or any tinge of disgust.

Instead, she only felt that wavering pleasure.

Her body had never come so hard, she didn't even know it was possible to feel what she just experienced.

After a few moments of reveling in that feeling, she got back on her feet.

There was no point cleaning herself up, it was Halloween.

Stella looked at herself in the mirror, black panties, a matching bra, and a whole lot of Ian's sweet, sweet blood — she looked delectable. *Hell,* she'd fuck herself right now.

Plenty of time for that later, babe

The demon that now used her body for its pleasure gave her a quick glimpse, an opportunity to see and *feel* what *they* had done together.

Stella stared at Ian's mangled corpse in the reflection of the mirror. Her eyes focused on the look on his face, the look that would be stained there forever, that look of hurt. Tears welled up in her eyes, she choked through desperate gasps for air.

She felt hollow. She killed him. She fucking killed him.

The parasite took its hold once more, letting out a maniacal laugh.

Jesus fucking Christ, stop the crying shit. We've only just started. A deal is a deal.

Seventeen years ago it wanted nothing more than to burn this fucking house to the ground, and tonight, it was damn well going to do just that. And it wasn't about to let that bitch get in the way, not again.

The moment Stella came hustling down the stairs, Nick eyed her with a grin, dancing with a red solo cup in hand. The liquid courage sloshed back and forth as he moved, at times spilling over onto the hardwood floor.

He was intoxicated, and the sight of his friend finally getting into the spirit only fueled that warm feeling.

"You look . . . fucking *fantastic*, babe. Where's . . . what's his name, oh yeah — eeeeeeeannnnn." Nick slurred his words, clearly more than just a few drinks deep now.

"Thanks Nicky-poo, Ian's taking a little nap."

Nick nodded and danced off in the opposite direction.

Stella watched as he disappeared into the crowd.

What a fucking cuck. Alright, princess, we've got shit to do.

Stella blended in perfectly with the crowds now. No one paid her any mind at all.

First, she set her eyes on the kitchen. Underneath the bathroom sink, she acquired a hammer and a torch lighter, both very important to its master plan.

The demon chose Halloween for a reason. It was just too easy to get away with anything it could imagine doing.

With her trusty tools in each hand, Stella made her way to the back door, one of two feasible exits.

Whoever built this place was an idiot. The raised structure offered a kickass garage and patio, but no low-set windows could lead to some problems.

Stella forced a key into the rusted keyhole. It was not the correct key, but rather a key that went to *who the fuck cares what.* After great force, the key finally crunched its way inside. The door was probably fucked enough, but for good measure, she gave the end of the key a good *wham* with the hammer, the silver stub now bent like an L.

Next on the list, the front door. She quickly decided she wouldn't mess with what worked, so she destroyed the other door almost identically to the last.

Finally, all that was left to do was to cut the power.

Was it necessary? Definitely not. But, it was Halloween so — might as well give them *you're in for a scareeee* vibes, or whatever.

They were all so drunk, they hardly noticed the music cutting to silence.

Stella plucked a half-empty bottle of vodka from the kitchen table that now acted as a bar. Without skipping a beat she downed half of what was left, saving the final few shots for the grand finale.

In the very corner of the living room, the entity and Stella took the entirety of the room in.

Everyone seemed to be having a *really* good time, all drunk, high, and horny. It was one hell of a party, Nick had a knack for that, she finally saw that now.

The *thing* let her forward for a moment.

She took that opportunity, screaming at the top of her lungs, "GET OUT!"

"*Oh nooo, get outttt, runnn rabbits, runnnnn little rabbits! — No one can hear you, nice try though.*"

Now in the doorway separating the kitchen from the rest of the house, Stella slipped her panties off, stuffing them into the neck of the liquor bottle.

If only we could watch them burn together, maybe you touch yourself to their pitiful screams, gotta keep us safe for now though, not done with you yet. After all, it ends with you, dollface. It started with a Barker, now it ends with one. That was the deal.

With the click of the torch, Stella lit one end of her sloppily folded panties. No one even saw it coming. In the state of a mad dash, she threw the bottle into the crowd of people, watching the room go up in flames, a beautiful chain reaction. Stella slammed the door shut behind her, locking and destroying any hope of survival.

From there it was either risk the jump, the *Dahmer* barbecue special, or the boring death of smoke inhalation.

Stella could hear the screams, the desperate cries for help, the gargled final words. Smoke trickled in from underneath the door. She wished it would be enough to kill her, but *it* wasn't going to let her off that easy.

Her hands pulled a large, recently sharpened butchers knife from the silverware drawer, slashing it through the air as if she were playing a nostalgic game of *fruit ninja*.

Instead of a fun game, without warning the knife came barreling down against the counter, taking her left pinky finger clean off with it.

This time, it let her feel the white-hot pain now surging through her nervous system. Blood sprayed against the granite countertop with the force of a newly installed faucet.

It hurt, it fucking hurt, she fought as hard as she could, but the hold was too strong, she couldn't push past it.

You mortals never do appreciate what you have. To think your dear old uncle put you in this position. He called to me many years ago, he woke me from my slumber. That prick wanted it all, a fate he was not destined for. Sucks he didn't listen to the nitty gritty fine print, that's what greed does to you, sweetie. It makes you oh so gullible, oh so stupid.

With another *wack*, her ring finger went flying, landing in the sink with a *thud*. Again she fought through the pain to no prevail, a pain so grave she wished it would just be done with her already and let her die.

Setting the pain aside for mere moments, a wave of rage overcame her. "You're telling me this shits happening because my dead uncle made some fucked up deal with the devil?"

"I am no devil, my essence predates that asshole. My true name does not translate to your mortal tongues, instead they refer to me as some pathetic bug. I am no bug, I am something far more sinister."

Stella listened to that self-ego-trip speech for another ten minutes.

Yada-yada-yada all-powerful being, blah-blah-blah blood-sucking demon, just the same useless pieces of information over and over again.

"So . . . you're like a vampire?"

Actually . . .

The creature was so distracted by its own rambling, Stella could feel it lowering its guard. It wasn't significant enough of a shift to break through, but with every ounce of fight that she had left in her, little by little her finger moved. It was a subtle movement, not enough to draw focus. But to her, it was everything.

So she let it talk, and talk, and talk and bask in the sweet stench of charred flesh that slowly filled the room.

She regained feeling of her entire hand, then soon after, her arm.

Incomprehensible screams for help eventually drowned out the demon's continued yapping. It was enough of a cover to slowly inch her right hand up against the cabinets, reaching for the handle to the area underneath the sink.

The door creaked open, it still didn't notice.

Her hand slipped inside, feeling around for anything that might help her.

Then by pure luck, and one of the very few perks of living with men, she felt the unmistakable shape of an electric penis pump.

In a eureka moment, she knew exactly what she needed to do. If she had full control, she might have actually squealed.

In one swift moment, she pushed the button activating the battery-powered suction, pressing the opening firmly around the grotesque duo of welts on her neck. If something found its way in, it had to be able to come out somehow — or at least that was the half-assed hypothesis she thought of on a whim.

The suction created between the bumps and the pump held strong, sucking what she hoped was demonic venom, or cum, or whatever substance it infected her with.

She could hear the faint *slosh* of it being milked out of her neck drop by drop.

Stella only had a few seconds before the Hatebug took notice. With the left side of her body that it still controlled, a serrated carving knife plunged deep into the very center of her stomach.

It was bad, but not a fatal blow, or at least not immediately.

The most likely scenario is that she would probably die of smoke inhalation before she succumbed to her blood loss.

With her left arm, the creature fought, grabbing at the peculiar device emptying her as if she were a juice pouch. It was no use, the vacuum seal held on.

As dark liquid now poured from the gaping wound across her torso, she could finally feel that deep feeling of hatred leaving her body.

"I fucking hate Halloween."

After

First responders arrived to the address of 37 *Abbott Road* late Halloween night. A 911 call had come in from 26-year-old *Jonah Clarke* who had been attending a party at the location in question. Through slurred speech, he stated to the operator, *"I don't know man, we're all getting fucking baked in here —"*

At the scene, police and fire & rescue discovered roughly eighty victims trapped inside the shell of a gruesome house fire.

Though the cause of the fire is currently unknown, detectives do suspect foul play.

There was only one survivor.

Unknown to the media, rescue workers found the young homeowner, Stella Barker barely conscious, but alive in the kitchen. She experienced great blood loss from a self-inflicted wound but is expected to make a full recovery. On the scene, she was heard reciting the same line over and over again, *". . . One bite is all it takes . . ."*

After discharge, it is believed she will be transferred to a long-term psychiatric facility until she is deemed mentally sound.

THE END . . . ?

SEE YOU NEXT HALLOWEEN, FUCKERS

Also by J.M. Gokey

Lantern

A weekend away in the middle of nowhere, sounds peaceful, right? Now add a lifetime of fear and a crazed stalker, what could go wrong?

Jen inherits her Grandmother's home in a rural town in Maine after her father passes away. Now she is forced to return to the place responsible for her childhood trauma.

At night a man has watched her for years — cigarette lit and lantern in hand. For years he has only watched from afar, until someone else gets in the way, tipping the scales.

The man decides it is time to take what he believes is his

Torch – Coming November 2024

The highly anticipated sequel to *Lantern*